Chapter 1
The day he took a stand

James started the day with not a care in the world. Riding his bike to school looking around taking in the sun on his face. Enjoying the spring fresh air and listening to his music on the way to school. He got to school with a smile on his face ready to start the day passing everyone saying "Hey what's up?" Then the school bully Chester was coming up to everybody and being annoying. It's like it gave him some sort of delight to be annoying. He started punching everybody in the arm and slinging his big belly into everyone knocking them into the lockers. James couldn't take it any more so James just ran to his classroom sitting at his desk with his chin resting on his hand daydreaming about the day that he would stand up to Chester. He envisioned in his mind his hair slicked back with sunglasses, a white t-shirt, a pair of jeans, and a coolness that radiated the whole hallway. He stood there sliding his sunglasses down his nose looking over the top of them at Chester. Then he said, " Hey man what is the problem?" Chester looked up and said, "N-n-nothing" with his head down. Then James moved closer to Chester bumping him with his hip and Chester tripped over someone's foot and went sailing down the hall on his belly sliding from side to side of the hallway. The next thing he knew the bell rang and class was over. Back to reality of this ginormous big bellied bully lurking around who knows where next.

The next period was gym class that just so happens Chester and James have together. Chester walks in stuffing a big twinkie in his mouth and starts messing with everyone as usual. He looks over at this one kid in their class that was very quiet and pushed him. Then he began making fun of another kid and then he spotted a girl in our class that everyone liked named Kimberly. He started pulling her hair and I began steaming, I mean what was wrong with this bully of a moose messing with the prettiest girl in school? Not knowing what else to do and being fed up with him I stood up and said, " Dude leave her alone everyone is tired of how you think you can mess with everyone and get away with it!" Chester then looked over at me like a bull ready to attack with his nostrils spread looking like Ferdinand moving closer and closer to me. I stood with my fist clenched and not knowing what I was gonna do as he got closer, but I could feel the heat rising of frustration in me. As he stepped right in front of me I knew it was now or never and I punched him with all my might I mean everything I had and he fell to the ground sliding across the gym floor. He looked up at me holding his jaw in amazement and said, " Man you hit me!" I couldn't believe what I had done and everyone being shocked along with myself included they began to cheer for me. Next thing I know the teacher is telling both of us to get to the office.

Both of us were taken to the principal's office and we both sat in that awkward silence staring at one another. After sitting there about twenty minutes the Principal came out and called us back and asked both sides of the story. Then he made us aware that our parents would be called to tell them that we had been fighting at school and it would then be decided what would happen.

Our parents arrived and after they all spoke to the Principal it was decided that because there was no fighting allowed in school that we would both be suspended for one week. The other thing they agreed on is that after being suspended when we came back we would have to sit next to each other in any classes that we have together. When I got home my parents sat down with me and asked exactly what happened because it was not like me to be fighting. So I started to explain that I just couldn't take it any more how he picks on everyone and he never gets in trouble. I felt like I was going to explode and that it wasn't right. I had been watching this all year and he would always make sure that it was a time when no one else was watching. I felt like someone had to take a stand against this bully. I told them that I was sorry for fighting, but I couldn't take it any more. After explaining to my parents they said that they appreciated my honesty, but they still didn't want me fighting that there is other ways to try to handle a situation like this. However, they did understand the reasoning in defending others. They explained that I would not be grounded, but during my suspension they wanted me to think about other ways to handle this for the future.

I layed there that night thinking about what had happened and I wondered why does Chester act the way he does and I knew there had to be more to the story than just wanting to be a bully. No one wants to be a bully really, Had Chester always been this way? I was really proud of myself how I had stood up to Chester *that day.*

Chapter 2
A Bullies Secret

The week had passed pretty quick and before I knew it we were back in school. I walked in that morning remembering what one of the rules would be when we came back from being suspended. We had to sit next to each other in any classes that we had together. I mean what were these adults thinking, how did they really think that this was going to work out? I know their thinking behind this was that Chester and I would work it all out and we would have to learn how to work with one another. In the real world this would be real nice, but I'm actually down here on Earth!

I walked into first period math class and sat at my seat. Then soon after Chester walked in and gave me a death stare as if his eyes were saying he was gonna kill me. He sat down next to me and turned to his side and when our math teacher Mrs. Jones came in she looked at Chester and told him he would have to face forward. So he finally turned around, but the whole time I could feel the heat rising between Chester and I. Class went ok and then when the bell rang we were leaving class and Chester came up and said." It's not over punk!" I turned around and stood there looking at him letting him know that I wasn't afraid of him. I walked on to my class and was going on with my day until I realized that my next period would be gym class and this was the next class that we had together. This should be very interesting! I walked in and went to change into my gym clothes and walked out onto the gym floor. There stood Chester and his best friend Larry. Of course they were staring at me and trying to intimidate me with their death stare. I ignored them and walked over to sit on the bleachers. We were waiting for Mr. Collins to come out and begin class. The anticipation grew as the whole class was thinking that something would happen because surely Chester was not going to let someone do him that way being the biggest bully in school. By this time it was going all around school that Chester and Larry had their heads together to get me. The whole time that we were in gym Larry and Chester would throw the ball as hard as they could at me during dodgeball and I was growing quite tired of it. It was starting to build with me and finally class was over and we all headed to the locker room to change clothes. I said to myself," Here it comes!" As I went to my locker I had a funny feeling and then when I opened my locker a bunch of balls came falling out. They busted up laughing thinking that this was just hilarious. This continued on all day with stupid little pranks that they thought were so funny. I knew he was just itching to start another fight and I was trying to ignore him. The day was just about over and we were headed towards the door to leave and here came Chester running up next to me with his spiky hair and the cheesiest smile that I had ever seen. Chester put his hand on my shoulder and said, " How did you like your first day back , did you get your welcome back message?" I looked at him and said," Get your hands off me" and he just laughed and went running out the door. I followed behind him out the door and was unlocking my bike when I looked up and seen this big tall guy there talking to Chester. He had grabbed him by his shirt and I stood back to see what was going to happen. He continued with his shirt in his fist and looked at Chester saying, " Come on Mom made me come get you, you little punk let's go, I always have to come get you! You think that I have nothing better to do than come and get you?" He finally let him go and had him get in the car. You could tell that this is where Chester was getting this from. He learned from the best how to be a bully.

        I kind of hung back and tried to follow them best I could and when I seen the street they turned on it was much to my surprise when I saw them turn just one block from my house. Did Chester live just one block from me? I continued on staying back as far as I could and I saw them pull into a driveway. I got off my bike and started walking and got behind a nearby bush. I watched them go inside and watched this older kid still running his mouth to Chester all the way in their house. When I turned around there stood a girl looking at me and said," So do you know them?" I said, " What are you talking about I had just stopped for a minute?" She looked at me and smiled, " Ok , but I saw you watching them." , she said. She stuck her hand out and said, " Hi I'm Shannon and I live here right down from those two goons that think they can beat up on everyone " and we shook hands.

She said." Ok so which one of them did something this time?" I looked at her with apprehension, but something about her I felt like I could trust her. I told her a little about what had happened and she said, "I can tell you exactly why Chester is the way he is. The bigger guy that was with him is his seventeen year old giant brother named Tim that always always picks on him and bullies him. We all have grown up on this street and he has always been so mean to Chester and now Chester thinks that he can be that way to other kids." I looked at her and suddenly it all made sense as to why he was this way. I said,"Thanks for the 411 I appreciate it." She smiled and said," Anytime and hey you didn't tell me your name." I looked back and said," Sorry it's James,, it was nice meeting you."

The rest of the week went on with Chester playing these stupid pranks on me. I actually felt kind of sorry for him because when he goes home Tim messes with him all the time and when he gets a break this kid decides to dish out what has been happening to him for probably most of his life. I had learned this bullies secret and I'm guessing this is why he treats people this way, but man you would think that he doesn't like it! It was finally Friday and this week was coming to an end, I watched Chester leave. He walked outside and there stood Tim again to get Chester and he put him in a headlock laughing as Chester's face turned red to the point where he was gonna explode. I watched as long as I could and finally I stepped up and said. "Hey, leave him alone!" Tim looked at me like he couldn't believe someone was talking to him this way. He said," Who is gonna make me?" He finally let Chester go and Chester stood in amazement as to why after all week him messing with me would I help him. I looked up at Tim remembering what Shannon had said what a giant he was. He looked like he was about seven feet tall. I looked at Tim and said, "You think just because you are big that you can pick on other people!" "Why don't you pick on someone your own size?" He grabbed me by my shirt and said."You little punk stay out of my business." He shoved me over in the grass and then I got up and grabbed a paper clip that I had earlier that day out of my pocket and I snuck behind the car and jabbed it in his tire. I told Chester to come on with me and we ran as fast as we could run.

Chapter 3
The mystery door

Chester was riding his bike and passed by James house. He saw James and Herbert outside and backed up. James asked Chester if he wanted to go to the beach with him and chester said "yes." When they got there James saw the little row boat that his family keeps there. James said, "There up ahead is our little row boat that we keep here at the beach. It gives my sister and I something to do when we come to the beach. I mean I know there is a lot to do, but we always take the boat out and pretend that we are going on adventures far off somewhere." Chester looked and James and gave him a smile and said,"That sounds cool!" As they continued walking James looked over at Chester and played dumb like Shannon had told him nothing asking, " So man I gotta ask why do you try to bully everyone?" Chester looked at James with a stare and then looked out at the ocean and sat down in the sand. James sat down beside him and said, " I understand if you don't want to talk about it." Chester looked back at James and had tears in his eyes, James thought could Chester be expressing emotion! Chester began "You see I have this older brother and he is always picking on me and always has. He always makes sure my mom and dad don't see how he is and then blames it on me. I am always in trouble and they think it's me, but it's not me! They just won't listen because it's their precious Tim." James looked at Chester and said, "I am sorry that has to be rough. Don't you see that if you do this to other people then it makes you just like Tim." Chester wiped his face and said, "I guess I see what you mean I just never looked at it like that. I mean it's all I ever knew and so I thought that was how you interact with others to get what you want or a good laugh for the day." James said, "You might actually find that you can make some great friends if you just lay off of the bullying. I mean think about how much better your life would be if Tim layed off." Chester smiled and said, "That would be great!" James stood up and reached out his hand to Chester to help him up from the sand and said, " Come on let's go on an adventure." The boy's both laughed and headed towards the boat. The boys stepped onto the boat and began to row, but as they got farther out the water started to turn purple. They were wondering why it was turning a different color. Chester asked James and James said "You can see it going around the mountain" and when they got around the mountain they saw a Door at the top of the mountain. They parked the boat on land and they started to climb up the mountain. Rocks started to come down the mountain and when they were coming down Chester yelled to James "Watch out Rocks!" They jumped into the water so the rocks would not hit them. Then they started to climb again and before they knew it they were almost at the top of the mountain. When they got to the top they saw the Door and it was glowing. When they opened the door it was like a garden obstacle course. Chester looked at James and said, "Should we go?" James said," let's do it! The boys began on this obstacle course of a garden and after a while seemed like they had been doing this for hours. They looked around and it looked like they were going into the jungle. James stopped for a minute and thought oh my goodness Herburt and looked down and up ahead and there sit Herburt waiting for James. He was relieved and felt bad all in the same because he had forgot about Herburt, but he was there keeping up with them.

As they stepped into the jungle they were hesitant because they didn't know what they were about to see or experience.

Chapter 4
The Jungle

They were in the midst of the jungle now and they came upon this dog just sitting there looking at them. James walked over and could see a dog tag on him, so he walked over and read his dog tag it said Tyson. They continued walking on and heard something from tree to tree and then in the bushes. They were getting a little freaked out as to what it was. Then to their surprise Tyson looked up at them and whispered, "Don't freak out that is only George." James and Chester screamed and Chester looked down at Tyson and said, "YYYYou just spoke why?" Even Herbert turned his head in amazement as to why this other creature that looked like a dog just like him was speaking. Tyson then looked up at Chester and said, "Why are you talking?" Chester continued on looking at him like he was going crazy. He looked at James and said, "Am I losing my mind, this dog is not talking to me!" James still in shock said, "Yeah man I think he did, I think." Herbert looking and trying to figure out what was going on then barked really loud as if he were giving it a try too. Tyson looked over at him and said," Give it up you mangy mut it will never work for you!" Then Tyson looked as if he smiled at them and said, "Come on this way."

After getting over the amazement of meeting Tyson a monkey came jumping down out of a tree and said,"So I see you met this guy and if you didn't know my name is George." The boys yelled again along with herbert in shock they all jumped backwards. James looked at Chester and said," I think we must of hit our heads." George looked at them and said, "Is it so hard for you to believe that animals are talking to you, maybe it looks weird that you guys are talking to us. Stick with us and we can lead you out of here, but it is all up to the two of you." Tyson and George began to laugh looking at James and Chester saying, " This is great they are really freaked out!" They decided as crazy as it sounded to follow their new found friends. Then as they were walking for what seemed like hours they came upon another dog that was coming out of some huge Elephant ears. He looked at them and said, " Hello fellows may I join you?" James looked at Chester and said, "Why am I not surprised now?" The boys said, "Sure why not come along." The new dog looked up at them and said," Thank you my name is Buster." They looked at him and said," Hey Buster." As they were walking Tyson said, "Up ahead you will see some ginormous over sized venus fly traps so don't let them get you, as it is lunch time." The boys listened and began to think what have we got ourselves into. They continued on through the sounds of bushes rustling and huge plants that you could only imagine existed. They were this beautiful shade of green and the flowers around them were the most beautiful vibrant colors of green, purple, red, and blues that they had ever seen. From time to time they would hear the trees and bushes moving around with the sound of monkeys all around them. After taking all of this in around them Buster looked at them and yelled, "Watch out and run!" The boys looked back and it was one of the giant venus fly traps reaching its long neck out to grab Chester and they yelled and ran so fast that they couldn't feel their feet hit the ground. As they were running then all of a sudden they tripped over this huge vine and fell right in a big mud puddle. The animals stood there looking at them like they didn't understand what just happened.

Right as they were getting up out of the puddle and had sat down on the ground they saw this snake come up right between them and said, " Are you alright boyssssss?" They could not believe that this really big snake was talking to them and they both passed out right there. George ran over and poured water on their faces and said," Boys come on you have to keep going." Then the snake looked at them and said, " By the way my name is SSSSSSally and when you get up walk up ahead, but don't turn left there is traps that way." The boys said,"ok". They continued on and all of their friends continued along with them. It was getting so hot and they felt like they really needed a drink to carry on. They saw a really clear stream and bent down to get a drink. Strange thing was the water looked like it was shaking and it was almost as if they could hear the rumbling of the moving ground. This sound was getting closer and closer, with water dripping down from James mouth he looked up at everyone else and said, " Dare I ask what is that sound and why is the ground shaking?" Tyson looked at them and said, "Run as fast as you can." They started to run, but here they were a whole herd of dinosaurs coming right at them as fast as they could come *at them. Their running was slower than the dinosaurs as they were right there on their heels, but they ran right past them towards this really big green looking bowling ball type of thing up ahead. Their hearts were still pounding almost out of their chest. Sally looked at the boys and laughed saying, "It is feeding time and they are headed to get that watermelon." The boys looked at her and said," Don't you think you could have told us before we almost had a heart attack?" Sally said," This was more fun."*

Chapter 5
The Journey continues

They continued walking on and started to see grapes lot's of grapes along with more and more dinosaurs. They continued on this grape trail that they had discovered and couldn't believe how many long neck dinosaurs they were seeing and just how green they were. The boys and their friends decided to take part in enjoying the grapes as the dinosaurs were. They had just went to reach for a grape and they saw a huge shadow coming in fast over them. When they turned to look around it was a big pink tongue and a gigantic wide open mouth that scooped them right up.

James and Chester along with all their friends except Sally found themselves sliding along with a lot of grapes down what seemed like a pink slide. They all went spinning and screaming " Ahhhhhhhh!" When they got to the bottom it was like a juicy river that they were now swimming around in. Chester looked at the others and said. "I think I'm going to be sick!" About that time he turned to one side and upchucked right there. George looked over and said, "How grrrrrrosssssss!" Chester looked at him and said," Shut up George" and continued to throw up. They all said, "Gross" and James said,"How are we gonna get out of this one?" Herbert started to bark and bark as if he was trying to say something to them all. Buster spoke up and said," We all have to remain calm and think. Sally is not here I know she will come up with an idea." They all tried to do just that and remain calm as more and more grapes splashed down into the grape river inside the dinosaurs's belly. All of a sudden with Chester continuing to upchuck in the dinosaurs river of grapes, stomach acid, and Chester's throw up it felt as if an earthquake was beginning to happen as they all started shaking all around. Then a big wind and the liquids inside the dinosaur started to spin uncontrollably like a tornado. They were all lifted up and went flying out the dinosaurs nostril from a sneeze.

They came flying out all slimy and went rolling and rolling until they hit a purple stream of water. They were all trying to get themselves together and James looked over at Chester and said," It's the water, the purple water!"

Chester said," It is, we are here we have to see where it leads to." James looked around and said, "I can't help, but wonder what happened for us to get out of the inside of that dinosaur?" Sally spoke up and said, "Help'ssssssss having friends out here in this place I used my tongue to tickle the dinosaur's nose and voila just like that you guys came flying out." They all laughed and said,"Thanks Sally." As they were trying to get out they looked down and saw purple fish swimming around them. They were all amazed at an actual purple fish. Buster looked up and said what they were all thinking, "Wonder what it tastes like?" Buster stood there for a moment with his head tilted and jumped back in and scooped one up in his mouth. The fish was flaping all around, but Buster started eating and said,"Mmmmmm quite yummy it tastes like grapes!" They looked at each other and thought, "A grape flavored fish?"

Everyone finally got out and started walking along the stream to see where it would lead. James was feeling a little hungry and was still seeing some grapes laying around. So he picked up one to eat and this little worm poked it's head out and said,"Please don't eat me!" James could not believe a little worm was talking to him and laid it down. He thought to himself," This place just gets weirder and weirder!" He then lost his appetite for the moment. They traveled on seeing more of the giant watermelons that they had seen earlier with the run in with the dinosaurs. Then they saw more giant fruits along the way with watermelons, cantaloupe, honeydew, pineapple, and the biggest strawberries they had ever seen. James picked a strawberry and looked it over very carefully to make sure there were no little friends poking out and then took a bite. To his surprise it was the juiciest and tastiest strawberry he had ever tasted. So he yelled to the others," Guys come and try these, you have to try them!" So they all came over and took part in trying these awesome strawberries. They all couldn't believe how they tasted. After getting pretty full on the strawberries they looked out and saw these beautiful flowers. It was a beautiful array of daisies, tulips, and lilies. They were the brightest reds, yellows, blues, and white colors they had ever seen. Then the fragrance was like that of a very fruity piece of fruit. It was the best smell that they had ever experienced. They noticed some of the bees were flying overhead and they began dropping their pollen. Only this pollen was purple. They walked into these *flowers and the pollen began to fall more and more making them feel very sleepy as they were walking and decided to take a nap for a while. So they climbed up the leaves on the stems of the daisies and laid down for a quick rest. Good thing they made it to the top when they did because their legs were feeling so weak. As they drifted off to sleep the petals fell over top of them as if it were a built in blanket to keep them warm. What will they wake up and find?*

Chapter 6
The buzzing adventure

They all started to wake up from one of the best naps they had ever had. As they were raising up and stretching their arms out they began to see a herd of bees flying towards them. Chester and James both were ducking and putting their arms up over their heads. They were bracing themselves as if they were going to be stung. They had frozen in this position and their faces were cringing with fright because these were the most over sized bees they had ever seen. Finally James looked up and there sat this bee just hovering in front of him in mid air smiling. James peeped through his arms and couldn't believe this bee was smiling at him. The bee looked at him and said," Come on we are gonna take you guys on a ride around this place, I think you guys will like it from our view!" So they all jumped up on the backs of the bees and they held on for the ride of their lives. They dipped, swooped, and ducked as they sped through the jungle, over top of the grape water river, the tons and tons of dinosaurs, the giant fruits, the beautiful waterfalls, and the biggest animals they had ever seen. They couldn't believe the view and how much fun this was. In all the excitement they saw something coming at them and the bee turned and said, "Hold on boys it's about to get interesting!" So the bees took off at a mighty speed and James and Chester along with all the animals held on with all their might as their cheeks flew back in the wind. Then the Pterodactyl bumped into the bees and made them fall into a stream of flowing gold. They came back up only to be knocked down again into the golden brick waterfall. When they fell to the bottom they got knocked out by the golden bricks.

After they came to and woke up from being knocked out they saw the bees flying over head as they were trying to make sure the Pterodactyls did not try to hurt them. They began waving to the bees and yelling for them. The bees came flying down and as they did the Pterodactyls were right on their tails. The bees had had enough and stopped in mid air and turned around shooting stingers at them like a machine gun. James and Chester could not believe what they were seeing. James looked to Chester saying ," Man, are they really shooting stingers at them like a machine gun?" Chester with his eyes glued on them and his mouth dropped said, "Yes they are!" Then they began to watch the Pterodactyls fall to the ground one by one to their death. All of the bees began cheering in delight as they protected themselves from the ferocious Pterodactyls. Then the bees came back down where James, Chester, and all their friends were and said," Now let's try this again, hop on!" So they all jumped back on flying around again and showing them where the golden river and the grape water meet. James asked the bees, "Why is there golden water, golden brick waterfalls, and the grape water? I mean what is up with that? The bee turned to James and said," You will see the story only gets more interesting from here." This had struck James interest and he began thinking what could the bee mean by that?

Chapter 7
Untold Secrets

The bees took them as far as they could and then landed in what looked like this golden city that was surrounded with the grape water. The bee looked at James and said," This is as far as we can take you guys, you will have to figure the rest out on your own." James looked at her and said, "Can you explain a little more?" She said, " All I can say is that there is this invisible force that won't let us into the secret place, you will have to figure this part out from here. Just know that many have tried, but never succeeded. The legend has it that long ago there was this native Indian chief that had a golden scepter. With this scepter it had magical powers that allowed him to do things that protected his family. One day this group of evil warriors tried to kill them and the chief used his scepter to create this invisible wall around their beautiful island. When he did this, he did it with such force that gold spilled out from the scepter making a golden stream and the gold brick waterfall. The grape water is his favorite drink and he wanted to leave this stamp on the land to let everyone know that it is their land by being his favorite drink. That is also why you see all the grapes and giant fruits. You see when he sent this force of protection out it also sent out other powers that allowed all the animals to talk and all the fruits to be oversized." James could not believe what he had just heard. James looked at Chester and all their friends and then back at the bee. "So what you are telling me is that we have to figure out how to get through, well I mean are there any clues?, James replied. The bee looked at him and said," Oh there are clues along with a lot of traps. So be very careful my friend." James looked to Chester, " Should we continue on?" Chester said," We have come this far."

So they continued on this unknown journey that they were all a little apprehensive about. The further they went they would see golden everything that weirded them out just a little bit. They saw this golden forest and they headed into it. They were thinking golden trees! Sally looked at them and said, " Remember there is no turning back once you enter the golden forest." They all looked at each other, James said, "We will all have to work together." They made a pact and started on this golden path in the forest. As they started walking they started to hear something that sounded like it was flying towards them. Tyson said,"You have awoken the warriors that protect the chief and his family." Then they heard something again and it was these flying arrows that were coming from all directions. So they all hurried up to the top of one of the golden trees and a magical card appeared that said," Continue if you dare and reach as high as you can?" James looked up and saw something shining above his head. He began to reach as high as he could. Then it was like this golden rope appeared where they could zipline across. So James went first and then the others jumped up onto this golden line and began ziplining across. After a couple of minutes it's like it just disappeared and they all went sailing into this swampy area of alligators. Buster said, "I have heard stories about this, you have to run quickly and stay on their heads. One slip and you are a goner!" So they all continued jumping across what seemed like twenty alligators. When they all had completed this task they sat down feeling like their hearts could explode at any moment. After they took a few minutes they looked around and saw a grape water pond with these golden toads inside hopping around. Something told James that this had something to do with the next task they must complete. The toad"s tongue would come in and out catching flies and in the next moment a golden bar flew into James hands from the toads mouth. He said," What am I supposed to do with this?" Sally replied with, "Try placing it on one of the lilypads, but be careful as if they touch you they are full of poison." So James went to place the golden bar on the lilypad and one of the toads tongues touched his arm. James let out this scream saying, "It feels like someone poured acid on my arm." Sally looked at him and said,"Hurry and put one of the golden leaves on your arm, it will ease the pain." So James listened and in a few seconds it was all better. Then he looked up and where he had laid the golden bar a staircase of lilypads appeared leading up to what looked like a big mountain of a rock. So they all followed James up this staircase to this big mountain of a rock. When they got up to the top it was a golden stone that had to be rolled away. When they looked at the rock these words appeared

ENTER IF YOU ARE A TRUE WARRIOR! Chester said,"No way a cave I'm not going in there!" James looked at him and said," We have come this far we have to." Chester looked at James, "I don't want to stay out here either." As they entered the cave they began to see drawings on the walls that showed the legend that the bee had told. James said,"It must be true." They continued further into the cave and could hear bats nearby and thank goodness they did not come near. They came to an area of the cave where they had to make a decision to go right or left. They went left and could hear a waterfall getting closer as they walked. Then they could see the most beautiful waterfall of grape water. As they got closer they looked over and there sat a little paddle boat to get into. So they got into the paddle boat and paddled under the grape waterfall, but when they got under that waterfall the water started rushing and sent them spinning round and round. Finally it sucked them into the middle and they were forced to swim for a few minutes before they could feel the edge of a rock. Chester reached up and it was an area to push up to. He said,"Come on guys over here." So they all pulled up to the area that Chester had discovered and before you knew it with the slippery rock they had fell into this whole that sent them sliding down a wet slide twisting and turning every which way that seemed like it lasted forever. When this slide finally spit them out they found themselves in the river of grape water. Chester floated to the top and said,"Wow, that was cool!" They all looked at him as if to say that he was crazy. Still inside the cave they swam over to the other side of this grape water where it looked like something shining at the other side. When they reached the other side there were all these beautiful colorful jewels at the bottom. James went for it as if something was pulling him towards the jewels. He swam down and went to pick it up as it was buried in the sand. He kept pulling until at last something like a metal concrete wall almost came around his hand and locked it in place. He was fighting and fighting under the water, but couldn't get his hand loose. Chester jumped in to try to help him and saw another jewel on the wall of the cave only this one was a lot bigger. Chester pushed on it with all his force with his foot as he held onto James. James became lifeless in the water from being under so long. Until finally it opened up and it sucked all the water under them as they were now in another whole room with these beautiful jewels everywhere.

When the others saw this happen they jumped down and into the room. Chester pulled James over as James was starting to cough from being under the water so long, but just thankful to be breathing air. Buster said,"Wow that was a close one don't you say." As James and Chester got up they began walking around and it was just room after room with all these jewels on the walls. They wondered what this was or what it used to be?" Sally looked at them with a glare and said,"You know noone has ever made it this far!" James looked at her and said," Tell us what else you know." She looked at him and said,"All in good time, all in good time!"

Chapter 8
The Paradise discovery

They continued walking on and found this room with a bunch of jewels, grapes, and water. Then amongst all of the other grapes they found some golden grapes laying in the mix. Sally looked at them and said,"If you find the golden grapes and eat it then you are the chosen one. You will be the king of grapes and you will be given superpowers that will allow you to go invisible." Tyson then ate the golden grape and he went invisible. Then he was looking around and eventually Tyson found this blue grape and Tyson ate it and he became giant size. All of a sudden they all fell into this big room. When they fell it's like they were all hovering in the air with this big force field. These six foot guys came out of these very tall doors and said,"Leave or we will be forced to hurt you!" Now the word big was an understatement in how big these guys were, they looked like they hit the gym every day! They had long black hair and these really big arms that had tribal tattoos all over them. They were carrying fire torches and had really deep voices. Chester whispered over to James,"Where did these guys come from?" James gave him a quick look and said,"Man I don't know, but I don't think this is good." They could hear Tyson, but still could not see him and his voice sounded much higher now. Tyson said,"Don't worry I got this!" These big warriors stood there looking all around trying to figure out where he was. Tyson lunged forward at them knocking them over and told the others to run, and to run as fast as they could. Tyson said,"I'll be fine go!" So the others took off, not even looking where they were going. Running and running as fast as they possibly could. They were all out of breath and could hardly breathe and they could see a light up ahead. So James and Chester yelled,"Come on guys I see it, there is a light up ahead and I think it's a way out." So they all sped up as fast as they could.

Before they could reach the light one of them must have set off something that caused a big rock to come rolling behind them. They could not believe how fast this thing was coming! They just had to speed up and *make it to the light up ahead. So closer and closer they came and finally they reached the outside. They could not believe what they were seeing! It was the most beautiful colors of flowers, even more beautiful than the ones they had seen before. Everything looked so fresh and new. There was this waterfall of grape water nearby, as well as a freshwater waterfall and then they saw this Native American Indian chief and a beautiful native girl standing near the grape waterfall. They did not know what to think. Is this the Indian Chief that they had been told about and did he think that they were there to harm them, James thought. James yelled over to them,"We come in peace and mean you no harm!" The Indian Chief and his daughter started walking towards them. Chester said,"Oh man I don't know if this is a good thing." They all stood very still and when he had reached them all the Indian Chief said,"I see that you have met my friends on your journey." James said,"Wait a minute you mean you all knew the Indian Chief?" They all looked up and smiled and said,"Yes." James and Chester could not believe what they were hearing. The Chief looked at them and said,"You see, a very long time ago there were some very bad warriors that had tried to come around and hurt us. We had to create some type of protection around our home. When you came through the rock in the beginning it was like I could feel an unfamiliar feeling and I sent all my friends out to see what or who was trying to come this way." The Chief looked at them and said,"So why have you come all this way?" James and Chester looked at each other and said,"Well we really were just trying to see where this grape water was coming from." The Chief laughed and said,"Ahhh yes the grape water it was kind of just our mark on this land, but I guess I didn't think about it striking the curiosity of others. Well, I'm sorry I put you guys through all this." They all looked around and James said,"Tyson, did he not make it out?" Tyson Barked and they still couldn't see him until the chief took his golden scepter and touched him and Tyson appeared. He was still a giant and the Chief said,"That will wear off." They all smiled and the chief invited them to come and eat a meal with them. So they all joined the Chief and his daughter around a fire for a very good meal. As they sat around the fire eating, the Chief shared more legends about their people from long ago. The boys were fascinated with all he shared with them and could not believe that this whole other world existed right there at the beach that they had been to so many times. Though the boys wanted to stay they knew that they had to go home. The Chief then took them to the grape waterfall and said,"If you just take this paddle boat under the waterfall you will find your way back." The boys thanked them for everything and got into the boat. James, Chester, and Herbert were on the boat and heading under the waterfall as they turned to say one last goodbye and just like that they went under the waterfall and it's like there was this rush of a feeling like it shut up and closed this invisible field into where they were. As they were going back to shore Chester said,"Did all this really just happen or was this some sort of dream?" James said,"No man it really happened, but you know that no one will ever believe this story.*

They went home that evening and when they got back it was like only a few hours had passed. To them it felt as though it had been days that they had been gone. This adventure had brought the boys together that summer and they were hanging out more than they ever thought they would. They would play baseball and visit each other. They came to find that they had a lot more in common than they thought that they ever would. I mean this changed something in Chester. He was actually a lot of fun to be around. He smiled and even laughed and told jokes. Chester had found a friend.

One night after playing baseball and just sitting there looking up at the stars James looked over at Chester and said,"Hey what's this I found something is in my pocket?" James reached in and pulled out a grape and the boys looked at each other and said,"AAAAAAAAAAAAAAAH!"

The End

The
Grape Waterfall
Adventure

www.ingramcontent.com/pod-product-compliance
Lightning Source LLC
Chambersburg PA
CBHW080732120726
48001CB00010B/3203